ONE MONDAY MORNING

ONE MONDAY MORNING

By Uri Shulevitz

Aladdin Books
Macmillan Publishing Company
New York

Collier Macmillan Publishers
London

ALADDIN BOOKS
an imprint of Macmillan Publishing Company
866 Third Avenue, New York, NY 10022
Collier Macmillan Canada, Inc.

One Monday Morning is also published in a hardcover edition
by Charles Scribner's Sons

First Aladdin Edition 1986

Printed in the United States of America

5 7 9 11 13 15 17 19   20 18 16 14 12 10 8 6 4

Library of Congress Cataloging-in-Publication Data
Shulevitz, Uri, 1935 —
One Monday morning.
(Reading rainbow book)
"An elaboration of the ancient French folk song 'Lundi matin, l'empereur,
sa femme. . .' " — T.p. verso.
Summary: The king and the queen and their growing entourage return
each morning to a tenement street until the little boy they have come to
visit is home to greet them.
[1. City and town life — Folklore.   2. Kings, queens, rulers, etc —
Folklore.   3. Folk songs, French]
I. Title.   II. Series.
PZ8.1.S5596On   1986   398.2'2'0944   [E]   85-28583
ISBN 0-689-71062-3 (pbk.)

To Ehud

One Monday morning

the king,

the queen, and the little prince came to visit me.

But I wasn't home.

So the little prince said,
"In that case we shall return on Tuesday."

On Tuesday morning the king, the queen, the little prince,

and the knight came to visit me.

But I wasn't home.

So the little prince said,
"In that case we shall return on Wednesday."

On Wednesday morning
the king,
the queen,
the little prince,
the knight,
and a royal guard
came to visit me.

But I wasn't home.

So the little prince said,
"In that case we shall return on Thursday."

On Thursday morning
the king, the queen,
the little prince,
the knight, a royal guard,
and the royal cook
came to visit me

But I wasn't home.

So the little prince said,
"In that case we shall return on Friday."

On Friday morning
the king, the queen,
the little prince,
the knight, the royal guard,
the royal cook,
and the royal barber
came to visit me

But I wasn't home.

So the little prince said,
'In that case we shall return on Saturday."

On Saturday morning
the king, the queen,
the little prince,
the knight, a royal guard,
the royal cook,
the royal barber,
and the royal jester
came to visit me.

But I wasn't home.

So the little prince said,
"In that case we shall return on Sunday."

On Sunday morning the king, the queen, the little prince, the knight, a royal guard,

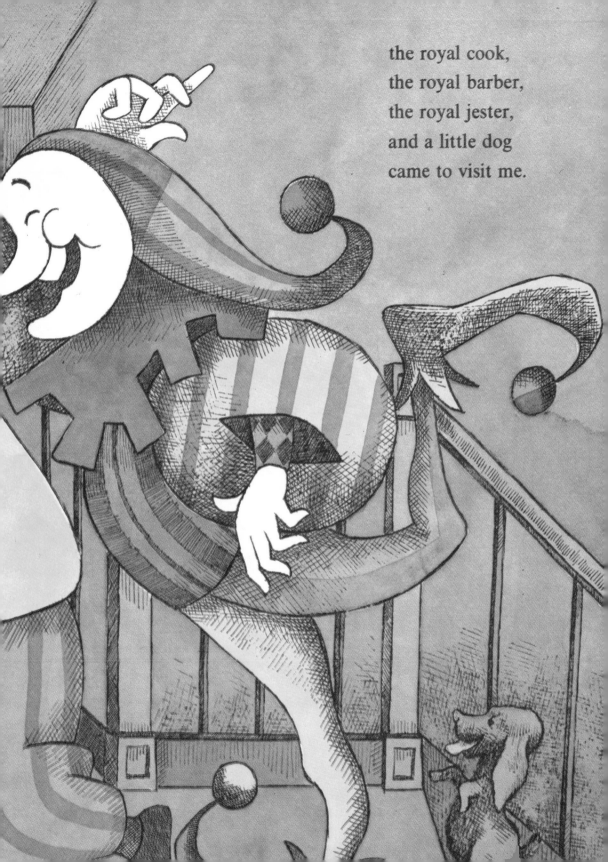

the royal cook,
the royal barber,
the royal jester,
and a little dog
came to visit me.

And I was home.
So the little prince said,
"We just dropped in to say hello."